The Kindness Quilt

Indigo Johnson

Tellwell Talent
www.tellwell.ca

ISBN
978-0-2288-8081-3 (Hardcover)
978-0-2288-8080-6 (Paperback)
978-0-2288-8934-2 (eBook)

Dedicated to a boy named Ryan and all the unicorns of the world
that have shown me what it means to be unconditionally kind.

Once upon a time there was a little green dinosaur. He was loved very much by his family and friends.

Little Dino wanted to see more of the world. He felt like he had a purpose and he needed to find out what it was.

So-LITTLE Dino went on a BIG adventure in the beautiful mountains. On his adventure he met lots of new friends. Everyone who encountered Little Dino loved his big heart.

One day, Little Dino got lost. He was frightened, but he knew that his family would search to the ends of the earth for him.

Daddy Dino used all his strength to lead the other animals on the search for his son.

Many neighbouring animals came to search.

Mommy Dino used all her courage to share stories about her son.

Animals from every place, near and far, came to search.

Creatures from around the world searched high and low for Little Dino.

Dragons flew over the snow-capped mountains and down into the valley bottoms, searching for clues with their keen eyes.

Mermaids scoured deep lakes and rushing rivers.

Fairies flitted through the dense green forest looking for any sign of Little Dino.

Creatures of all shapes and sizes joined Little Dino's family in the mountains to search for him, but he was nowhere to be found.

Early one morning, a beautiful unicorn came to the mountain where Little Dino had disappeared. She shared *The Legend of the Kindness Quilt* to the crowd that was quickly gathering around her.

"All those lost will be found," she told them.

"Sometimes, they just need a little extra light to find their way home. When you share in an act of kindness, the world gets brighter and more beautiful. As patches of kindness are added to this," she continued, pulling out a small patchwork quilt that was glowing softly, "the light will get brighter and that light will guide the lost home."

The creatures all got to work.

Bear shared his den to shelter the homeless.
Owl shared her wisdom to guide the confused.
Fox shared her intelligence to teach the uneducated.

The quilt began to grow, and the light from it shone brighter.

Rabbit shared his joy to heal the broken-hearted.
Wolf shared her strength to protect the vulnerable.
Moose shared his crown to support the weak.

The quilt grew bigger, and its light started to spread across the world.

Squirrel shared his stash to feed the hungry.
Bird shared her song to cheer the sad.
Stag shared his boldness to encourage the shy.

Animals near and far added their own piece of kindness to the patchwork quilt.

Soon the entire world was wrapped in the warm embrace of the colourful quilt. Each square added its own piece of light to the world.

There was only one more thing to do to bring Little Dino home.

The unicorn bowed her head and touched her silver horn to the quilt. A ripple of light spread across the globe. Kindness and her warmth touched the hearts of all Mother Earth's children.

Little Dino looked up from where he was and saw the bright light. Now he knew where to go. No longer feeling lost, he headed towards the warm glow.

Along the way, he was amazed to see so many creatures all giving of themselves.

Bird singing her cheerful tune,
Squirrel sharing his winter stash and
Wolf standing strong, protecting those most vulnerable.

Little Dino had at last found his purpose.

Even in his absence, he had shown other creatures, great and small, that they have the ability to share kindness with friends and strangers. He smiled softly as he continued to the front of the crowd where he found his sisters and Mommy and Daddy Dino awaiting his arrival.

At long last, Little Dino reunited with his family and friends.

It wasn't just Little Dino who was reunited with his loved ones because of the kindness of complete strangers.

Just as the unicorn had promised, all those lost were found that day and the world continued to grow into a brighter and more beautiful place.

Ryan Shtuka (Missing since February 17, 2018 - Sun Peaks, BC)

On February 16, 2018, twenty-year-old Ryan Shtuka attended a house party in the ski village of Sun Peaks, British Columbia, where he had been living and working for two and a half months. He left the party in the early morning hours of Saturday, February 17, to walk the short distance home. Ryan has not been seen since.

What followed was an extensive search effort led by local law enforcement and Search and Rescue crews. When Ryan remained missing after these teams had completed their efforts, Ryan's parents, Heather and Scott, and his two younger sisters were left to their own devices to continue searching for him in vast mountain terrain. On February 17, the day Ryan was last seen, Heather and Scott had driven the nine hours from their home in Beaumont, Alberta, to Sun Peaks to begin their search for him. They did not return home until June 19, over four months later.

Record amounts of snow fell on the mountain that winter, and in many areas, it did not melt until late May. Scott searched every single day. Determined to find his son, he tore apart snowbanks and led searches through dense forested areas for four months straight. Heather, although healing from surgery, oversaw the command centre coordinating volunteers. She made news and media appearances and gained a large social media following by blogging about Ryan, their search efforts, and her grief process throughout this tragedy. In an early blog, Heather wrote about Ryan's childhood love of dinosaurs and the colour green; a green longneck dinosaur thus became a symbol of his story.

Ryan's disappearance and the search efforts took social media by storm, and a following of this story quickly developed. Today, Ryan's Facebook page has over thirty-thousand members. Local community members from Sun Peaks and surrounding areas, friends, and strangers from Ryan's hometown, and volunteers from across British Columbia and Alberta flooded the mountain to help. The search soon developed into methodical grid searches with hundreds of volunteers searching daily while contending with snow depths of over ten feet.

The most unexpected outcome of Ryan's disappearance and this awful tragedy is a beautiful community of love, support, and hope that blossomed around the Shtuka family. Meal trains, fundraisers, and donations flooded in. Buses, flights, and hotels were donated for search efforts. Boxes of food and supplies came to the command centre for the family and volunteers. Every single day for months, volunteers showed up at the command centre to join the search efforts. People hung posters around the village and surrounding communities and shared Ryan's story through social media. Lifelong friendships were forged.

For Ryan's twenty-first birthday, exactly one month after his disappearance, a Random Act of Kindness campaign began. Supporters were encouraged to share an act of kindness in Ryan's memory along with his picture in their community. These acts included such gestures as buying a coffee for someone or leaving a friendly note on the car beside you in the parking lot. Random acts of kindness were soon shared across the globe in Ryan's name.

From the depths of great loss and tragedy, kindness prevailed.

Despite the intense search efforts that continue to this day, no sign of Ryan has been found. Heather and Scott continue to make monthly trips to Sun Peaks where they find peace in being in a place where Ryan found so much joy. They continue to organize search efforts as weather conditions permit.

You are welcome (and encouraged) to share in a random act of kindness in Ryan's memory and tell his story.

To learn more about Ryan's disappearance, to join a search or to donate to the cause you can visit www.findryanshtuka.com. You can also find his Facebook community at "Missing: Ryan Shtuka." Heather Shtuka's memoir *Missing from Me* recounts the first year of searching and the love and loss she has experienced since Ryan disappeared. *Missing from Me* can be purchased on Amazon.

Ten percent of all proceeds of this book will be given to the Free Bird Project. This non-profit organization, co-founded by Heather Shtuka, provides resources, skills, and loving support to families of missing persons. To learn more about this organization, visit www.thefreebirdproject.com or join their community on Facebook at "The Free Bird Project."

THE **FREE BIRD** PROJECT

Christmas 2017 (Shortly before Ryan moved to Sun Peaks, BC)

Heather Shtuka organizes volunteer searchers (May 2018)

Scott Shtuka at Sun Peaks (February 2018)

Volunteers at Sun Peaks (April 2018)

The search continues (October 2019)

Indigo distributing Missing Ryan Shtuka posters at Sun Peaks, BC (November 2018)

About the Author

Indigo is an elementary school teacher who grew up with an immense love for books. She enjoys reading her childhood favourites with her students and finds joy in teaching lessons that encourage kindness and build a sense of community.

The Kindness Quilt reflects on the beautiful community of love, support, and kindness that arose around the Shtuka family after Ryan's disappearance in the small community of Sun Peaks, British Columbia, a short distance from Indigo's hometown. She joined search efforts and met Ryan's family in the early days of his disappearance. She continues to be involved in search efforts to this day.

Through this immense tragedy, Indigo developed lasting friendships with Ryan's family and other followers of Ryan's story. *The Kindness Quilt* began as a university project and developed into the book you hold today. Its purpose is to encourage you to offer kindness towards strangers and loved ones, and to share Ryan's story.

"Leave footprints of love and kindness on every
step of your journey" - Winnie the Pooh

CPSIA information can be obtained
at www.ICGtesting.com
Printed in the USA
BVHW090551210223
658739BV00024B/124